GLOW IN THE DARK

Brillando En La Oscuridad

Book #2
Created & Written By Sam Feldman & Enrique C. Feldman
Illustrated By Abraham Mendoza

Follow Your Curiosity

www.SamTheAnt.com

for Children's Books, Brainwave Games, and Music!

samtheantofficial@gmail.com

@samdantofficial

To all the parents and their children, to all the smiles, hugs, and dreams which they share. To the dreamers: to all the dreams that were and that will be. To the everlasting creative spirit burning inside every dreamer. Keep dreaming, creating... exploring.

Thank you Nick Feldman for your love, belief and inspiration as these stories were created. You embody many of the positive traits found in all of these books.

Sam and Sandy felt grateful as they flew on Drag's back. Because of Drag's help, they had escaped the flood!

Sam y Sandy se sentían agradecidos mientras volaban encima de la espalda de Drag. Con su ayuda, habían escapado la inundación!

"I miss the colony," said Sandy.

"We could always turn around and go back home," said Sam.

Sandy frowned and looked off into the distance, feeling very conflicted. "No...if we turn back now, I'll always regret not finding out what else is out there," said Sandy. "We'll go back one day, but for now, let's keep flying."

"Extraño a la colonia," dijo Sandy.

"Siempre podemos volver a casa," dijo Sam.

Sandy frunció el ceño y miró a lo lejos, sintiéndose muy en conflicto. "No ... si vuelvo ahora, siempre voy a lamentar no haber buscado mas en la vida," dijo Sandy. "Volveremos un día, pero por ahora, vamos a seguir volando."

What does it mean to feel conflicted?

¿Qué significa sentirse en conflicto?

They kept flying north and the sun began to set. They noticed changes in the colors and shapes below them.

Siguieron volando hacia el norte con la puesta del sol. Se dieron cuenta de los cambios en los colores y formas por debajo de ellos.

What shapes do you see?

¿Qué formas ves?

"Night is coming soon," said a sleepy Drag.
"There's the moon," yawned Sandy.
"And the twinkling stars," added Sam.

"La noche viene pronto," dijo Drag, que estaba cansado.
"Ahí está la luna," bostezó Sandy.
"Y las estrellas brillantes," dijo Sam.

"I'm doing my best to keep flying," said Drag. "But my wings are exhausted!" Sam and Sandy were starting to doze off as well. They had just begun their descent when Sam noticed a glowing golden light in the distance.

"Estoy luchando para seguir volando," dijo Drag. "Pero mis alas están agotadas!" Sam y Sandy estaban empezando a quedarse dormidos tambien. Estaban bajando cuando Sam notó una luz brillante en la distancia.

"What is that?" asked Sam, nudging Sandy awake.

"I don't know..." said Sandy.

Drag frowned, squinting at the light. "It's pretty fuzzy from here. I can't make it out!"

"¿Qué es eso?," Preguntó Sam, ayudando a Sandy despertar.

"No sé ..." dijo Sandy.

Drag entrecerró sus ojos a la luz. "Es bastante difícil ver desde aqui!"

As they flew closer to the source of the light, they could see it more clearly: a monstrous, glowing creature, which seemed to be hovering above the ground! But what kind of giant animal could glow in the dark?

Mientras volaban más cerca a la luz, podían ver la forma más clara: un animal brillante, que parecía estar flotando sobre el suelo! Pero, ¿qué clase de animal gigante podría brillar en la oscuridad?

What kind of animal glows?
¿Qué tipo de animal es tan fosforescente?

"What is that thing?" Sandy whispered apprehensively.
"I don't know," said Sam.
"Maybe we should turn around," said Sandy, beginning to panic.

"¿Qué es esa cosa?" Sandy susurró con aprensión.
"No sé," dijo Sam.
"Tal vez deberíamos volar en una dirección diferente," dijo Sandy, que estaba comenzando a entrar en pánico.

"Wait!" said Sam. "Remember when we first met Drag? We were scared because Drag was different from us. This new creature could help us, just like Drag did!"
"Hear, hear!" Drag exclaimed in agreement.

"¡Espera!" Dijo Sam. "¿Recuerdas cuando conocimos a Drag por primera vez? Teníamos miedo porque Drag era diferente. Esta nueva criatura nos podría ayudar, como hizo Drag!" "De acuerdo!" exclamó Drag.

The trio kept flying...then suddenly, the monstrous, glowing creature exploded!

They found themselves surrounded by thousands of tiny, glow- in-the-dark...

El trío siguió volando ... y de pronto, el animal brillante explotó!

Se encontraron rodeados por miles de pequeñas y fosforescente ...

Why did the creature explode?
¿Por qué explotó la criatura?

"Fireflies!" Drag exclaimed with a wide smile.
"Wow! They're beautiful!" Sam exclaimed. Drag nodded, but then yawned and started to drift off to the right before making a sharp downward dive.

"Luciérnagas!" exclamó Drag con gran sonrisa. "¡Maravilloso! Son preciosas!" exclamó Sam. Drag asentió, pero en ese momento bostezó y comenzó a desviarse hacia la derecha antes de comenzar a bajar en picada.

"Drag, look out!" Sandy cried as they plummeted toward the ground.

"Drag, cuidado!" gritó Sandy, mientras comenzaban a caer en picada hacia la tierra.

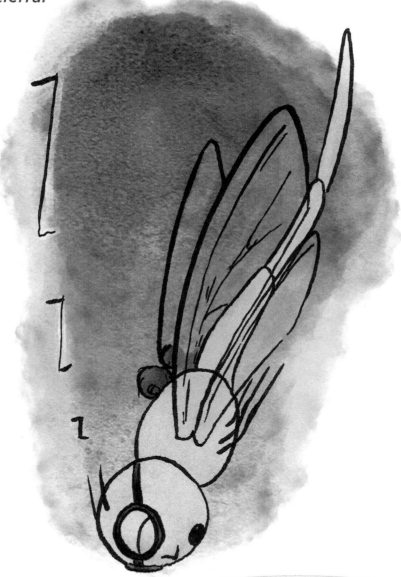

What is happening to Drag? Why?
¿Qué está pasando con Drag? ¿Por qué?

Then something amazing happened! The fireflies quickly flew underneath Drag, Sam, and Sandy, and linked arms, creating a net with their bodies! Working together, the fireflies carried them onward as the moon appeared larger in the sky.

Then the fireflies began to sing...

¡De repente algo increíble sucedió! Las luciérnagas volaron rápidamente por debajo de Drag, Sam, y Sandy, con brazos atados, creando una red con sus cuerpos! Trabajando juntos, las luciérnagas los cargaron mientras siguieron volando con la luna agrandando en el cielo.

Las luciérnagas comenzaron a cantar ...

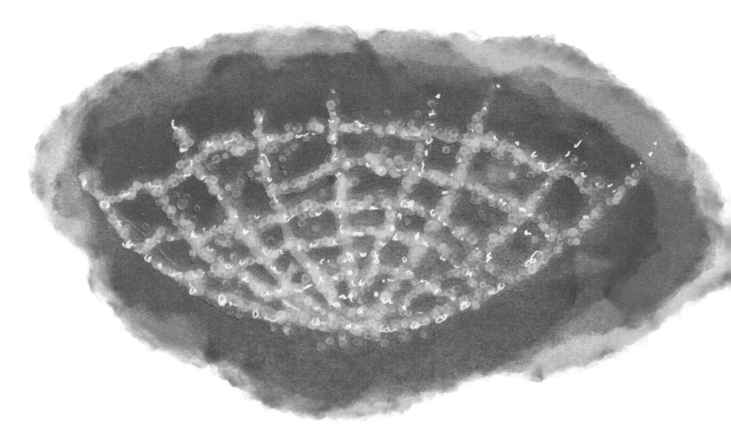

"Night is coming soon,
carrying the moon.
Stars appear, mother's near,
singing this tune."

*"Va llegando la noche,
cargando la luna.
Estrellas aparecen, mamá esta cerca,
cantando esta melodía."*

As the moonlight reflected off the Red Rocks, the fireflies continued singing:

"Close your sleepy eyes.
Hear sweet lullabies.
Clouds that float
like a boat
fill up the sky."

Con la luz de la luna reflejando en las rocas rojas, las luciérnagas siguieron cantando:

*"Cierra tus ojos cansados.
Escucha la dulce melodía.
Nubes que flotan
como un barco
llenando el cielo."*

The fireflies descended into a forest as they continued their lullaby:

> "Rest your weary head
> on a soft warm bed.
> Dreams may bring anything;
> your heart's being fed."

Las luciérnagas descendieron en el bosque mientras continuaban su canción de cuna:

> *"Descansa tu cabeza cansada*
> *en una cama suave.*
> *Los sueños pueden traer cualquier cosa;*
> *alimentando tu corazón."*

Drag, Sam, and Sandy were tucked into a bed of grass with a leaf blanket at the foot of a tree. They could hear the trickling water of a nearby creek as the final words of the lullaby swept them off to sleep:

Drag, Sam, y Sandy estaban en una camita de pasto con una cobija de hojas cerca de un árbol. Podían oír el agua goteando de un arroyo cercano, mientras las últimas palabras de la canción de cuna los pusieron a dormir:

Who made the bed for Drag, Sam, and Sandy?

Why?

¿Quién le preparó la cama a Drag, Sam, y Sandy?

¿Por qué?

17

"Dreams can set you free
to fly with wings, you see.
Planets spin, invite you in,
and just let you be."

"Los sueños pueden liberarte
si con alas vuelas, verás.
Los planetas giran, te invitan,
y te dejan ser."

18

When they woke up in the morning, they could still hear the gentle creek not far off, and they could feel the warm sun streaming through the canopy of leaves high above them. After a moment, they noticed that the fireflies had left them a note!

Cuando se despertaron por la mañana, todavía podían oír el agua del suave arroyo que estaba cerca, y podían sentir el calor del sol que entraba por las hojas del bosque. Después de un momento, se dieron cuenta de que las luciérnagas les habían dejado una nota!

"Go north to see a true wonder of the world, and tell the Rappin' Rabbit we said hello. May you always be guided by light."
- The Fireflies

"Vayan hacia el norte para ver una verdadera maravilla del mundo, y digale al Conejo Rappin que le mandamos saludos. Que siempre sean guiados por la luz."
- las luciernagas

"What is this wonder of the world?" Sandy asked.
"There's only one way to find out," said Sam.
Drag nodded in agreement and said, "Time to fly!"

"¿Qué es esta maravilla del mundo?" preguntó Sandy.
"Sólo hay una manera de saberlo," dijo Sam.
Drag asentió con la cabeza y dijo: "Es hora de volar!"

As they soared north over the Red Rocks of Sedona, Arizona, Sam thought out loud,
"Wow, the world sure is beautiful...just think how much we haven't seen!"
"I can't wait to keep exploring!" said Sandy.
"You won't have to wait much longer," said Drag. "I have a feeling something amazing is waiting for us!"

Mientras ascendieron hacia el norte sobre las rocas rojas de Sedona, Arizona, Sam pensó en voz alta,
"Guau, el mundo es hermoso ... imagínate todo lo que no hemos visto!"
"Estoy ancioso por seguir explorando! dijo Sandy.
"No tendrán que esperar mucho más tiempo," dijo Drag. "Tengo la sensación que nos espera algo incredible!"

THE END and a beginning
FINAL y principio

*Lyrics from the song "Night" with permission by Alice Pringle from her children's album "Kaleidoscope" available online at www. alicepringle.com

*Letras de la canción "Night" con permiso de Alice Pringle del álbum infantil "Kaleidoscope" disponible en línea en www.alicepringle.com

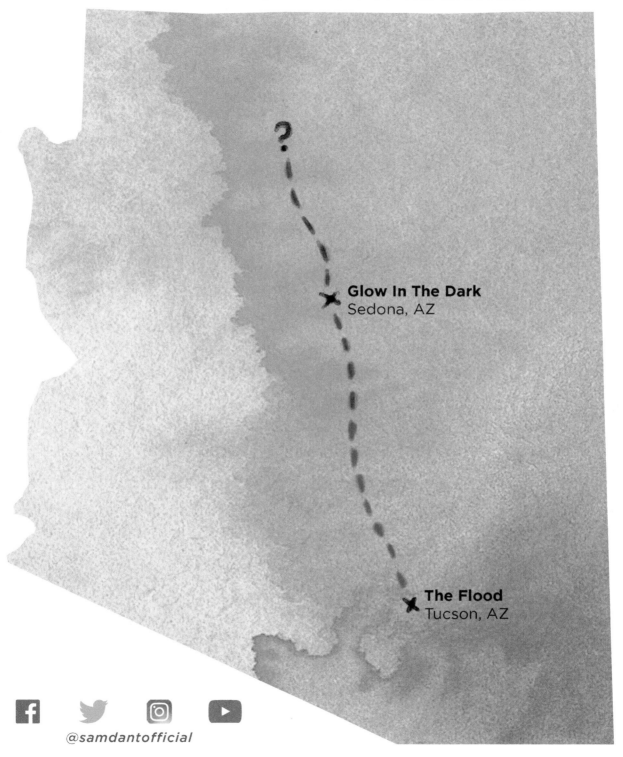

Glow In The Dark
Sedona, AZ

The Flood
Tucson, AZ

LEARNING GUIDE

THE ART OF THE QUESTION

This learning guide is created in a way to help you extend the learning from this story. Some of the keys for this to take place are:

- What kinds of questions do you ask your children?
- Do you allow enough silence after the question (the sound of thinking) for authentic responses
- to come forth?
- Do you ask more questions or do you make more statements?

The Art of asking a question also involves the quality of how you ask the question, including your facial expressions and body language. Here are just a couple of sample questions you could ask. The key is making sure to ask "Why?"

- How did Sam and Sandy feel about Drag when they first met in book one? Why?
- How did the relationship between the ants and the dragonfly change? Why?

GUÍA DE APRENDIZAJE

EL ARTE DE LA PREGUNTA

Esta guía de aprendizaje le ayuda a ampliar el aprendizaje de este cuento. Algunas de las claves importante son:

- ¿Qué tipo de preguntas les hacen a sus niños?
- ¿Permita suficiente silencio después de la pregunta (el sonido de pensamiento) para dejar
- tiempo para respuestas auténticas?
- ¿Haces más preguntas o haces más declaraciones?

El Arte de hacer una pregunta también implica la calidad de cómo hacemos la pregunta, incluyendo sus expresiones de cara y cuerpo. Aquí hay unos ejemplos de preguntas que podrías hacer. Es importante preguntar "¿Por qué?"

- ¿Cómo se sintieron Sam y Sandy de Drag cuando se conocieron en el primer libro? ¿Por qué?
- ¿Cómo cambió la relación entre las hormigas y la libélula? ¿Por qué?

PARENT GUIDE

READING TO YOUR CHILD

CHARACTER DEVELOPMENT

Each time you are storytelling, consider focusing on the perspective of a specific character. In this case, what kinds of questions would you ask from the perspective of:

• Sam the Ant
• Sandy the Ant
• Drag the Dragonfly

What kinds of questions would Sam, Sandy and/or Drag ask?

PHYSICAL ENVIRONMENT

What kinds of questions can you ask the children about the physical world the Ants live in? Perhaps questions about the weather, the land, and the sky? How does the physical environment impact the ants, the dragonfly, and the story?

RE-TELLING THE STORY

One important goal to strive for is for the child to re-tell the story with words, actions, drawing, painting, clay, etc. Beyond that goal would be for the child to tell the adult the story and ask their own questions related to the story.

GUÍA DE LOS PADRES

LEYENDO A SU NIÑO

DESARROLLO DE PERSONAJE

Cada vez que estas compartiendo un cuento, considera concentrarte en la perspectiva de un personaje específico. En este caso, ¿qué tipo de preguntas harías desde la perspectiva de:

*   La hormiga Sam
*   La hormiga Sandy
*   La libélula Drag

¿Qué tipo de preguntas harían Sam, Sandy o Drag?

ENTORNO FÍSICO

¿Qué tipo de preguntas puedes hacer a los niños sobre el mundo físico de las hormigas? Quizás preguntas sobre el clima, la tierra y el cielo? ¿Cómo el ambiente físico afecta a las hormigas, la libélula y el cuento?

REPITICIÓN DEL CUENTO

Un objetivo importante es invitar al niño a contar el cuento de su perspectiva con palabras, acciones, dibujo, pintura, etc. Más allá de esa meta sería mejor si el niño le lea el cuente al adulto y haga sus propias preguntas relacionadas a este cuento.

OUR CO-AUTHORS

Sam Feldman is a vocalist, conductor, producer, and student at the University of Arizona, where she studies music and creative writing. She works as a children's choir director and afterschool music teacher at St. Philips in the Hills Episcopal Church and currently serves as President of Enharmonics A Cappella, with whom she recently performed for Gabrielle Giffords. Sam also performs locally with the Tucson Symphony Orchestra, The Helios Ensemble, Audivi Vocem, and the Tucson Girls Chorus Alumnae Choir.

Enrique C. Feldman is a world renown educator and performing artist. He is involved in elevating how children learn as the Founder and the Director of Education for the Global Learning Foundation. Enrique is the adaptive editor and Director of Education for Make a Hand, a producer of children's music, a two-time Grammy Nominated Artist, a Redleaf Press Author, and the creator of iBG (Intellectual Brain Games). Additionally, Enrique is the co-creator of the theatrical productions "Dancing in the Universe" and "The Inner Journey."

Abraham Mendoza is an up and coming illustrator who is a designer and illustrator for Art Mine Design in Tucson, Arizona. Having studied graphic design at Pima Community College, Abraham is the illustrator of the children's book "We're all Green on the Inside" by Jenna Stone. He is known for his work in Brand Development, Website UI design, illustrative design, and creative Art direction.

*Follow Your Curiosity at www.SamTheAnt.com
for Children's Books, Brainwave Games, and Music!*

samtheantofficial@gmail.com

@samdantofficial

CPSIA information can be obtained
at www.ICGtesting.com
Printed in the USA
LVOW05s1255151017
552516LV00034B/227/P